Bippo and Boppo

First published in 2008
by Wayland

Text copyright © Penny Dolan 2008
Illustration copyright © Bruno Robert 2008

Wayland
338 Euston Road
London NW1 3BH

Wayland Australia
Level 17/207 Kent Street
Sydney, NSW 2000

Series Editor: Louise John
Editor: Katie Powell
Cover design: Paul Cherrill
Design: D.R.ink
Consultant: Shirley Bickler

A CIP catalogue record for this book is available from the British Library.

ISBN 9780750255356

Bippo and Boppo

Written by Penny Dolan
Illustrated by Bruno Robert

WAYLAND

Bippo was a new clown
in Carlo's circus.

He was very short.

Boppo was a new
clown, too.

He was very tall.

5

"Welcome to my circus!"
said Carlo. "Do you have
any good tricks?"

"Yes," said Bippo.

"We have lots of funny tricks," said Boppo.

At the show, people smiled at Bippo and Boppo's tricks but they did not laugh.

"You need to be much funnier," said Carlo.

"You must do some new tricks."

Bippo and Boppo stayed
up all night.

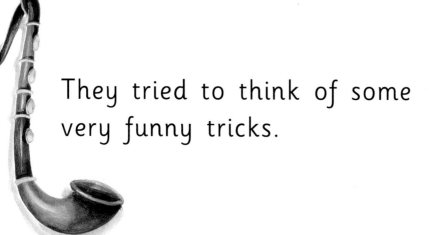

They tried to think of some
very funny tricks.

The next morning, Bippo and Boppo were so, so tired.

"We must have a nap before the show starts," said Bippo.

"Wake up, Bippo!
Wake up, Boppo!"
shouted Joey the Juggler.

"The crowd is waiting!"

Quick! Bippo pulled on
a clown suit.

It felt very tight!

Hurry! Boppo pulled on
a clown suit.

It felt very baggy!

They ran into the ring and
began their clown tricks.

Then they saw each other.
How silly they looked!

Bippo was in Boppo's big suit! Boppo was in Bippo's small suit!

How funny they looked.

Everyone laughed and laughed.

"Well done, you two!"
cried Carlo. "You can be
in my circus show anytime!"

23

START READING is a series of highly enjoyable books for beginner readers. **The books have been carefully graded to match the Book Bands widely used in schools.** This enables readers to be sure they choose books that match their own reading ability.

Look out for the Band colour on the book in our Start Reading logo.

The Bands are:

Pink Band 1

Red Band 2

Yellow Band 3

Blue Band 4

Green Band 5

Orange Band 6

Turquoise Band 7

Purple Band 8

Gold Band 9

START READING books can be read independently or shared with an adult. They promote the enjoyment of reading through satisfying stories supported by fun illustrations.

Penny Dolan had great fun writing about Carlo's Circus, because she could pretend she was an expert juggler, brave trapeze artist, cheeky clown and an amazing elephant rider – even though she's definitely not!

Bruno Robert lives and works in Normandy, France, where he was born. He always wanted to draw and play with colours. When he is illustrating a story like this one, he likes to think of a bright and colourful world that is full of humour.